600

LIBRARY
ANDERSON ELEMENTARY SCHOOL

W9-DJQ-249

A NOTE TO PARENTS

When your children are ready to "step into reading," giving them the right books is as crucial as giving them the right food to eat. **Step into Reading Books** present exciting stories and information reinforced with lively, colorful illustrations that make learning to read fun, satisfying, and worthwhile. They are priced so that acquiring an entire library of them is affordable. And they are beginning readers with a difference—they're written on five levels.

Early Step into Reading Books are designed for brand-new readers, with large type and only one or two lines of very simple text per page. **Step 1 Books** feature the same easy-to-read type as the Early Step into Reading Books, but with more words per page. **Step 2 Books** are both longer and slightly more difficult, while **Step 3 Books** introduce readers to paragraphs and fully developed plot lines. **Step 4 Books** offer exciting nonfiction for the increasingly independent reader.

The grade levels assigned to the five steps—preschool through kindergarten for the Early Books, preschool through grade 1 for Step 1, grades 1 through 3 for Step 2, grades 2 through 3 for Step 3, and grades 2 through 4 for Step 4—are intended only as guides. Some children move through all five steps very rapidly; others climb the steps over a period of several years. Either way, these books will help your child "step into reading" in style!

Amelia Earhart
Given by her
Mother
1940

Step into Reading™

VANISHED!

The Mysterious Disappearance of
Amelia Earhart

By Monica Kulling

Illustrated by Ying-Hwa Hu
and Cornelius Van Wright

A Step 4 Book

Random House New York

Photo credits: AP/Wide World Photos, 6, 10, 21, 27, 46, 48; Corbis-Bettmann, 14, 15, 17, 18-19, 22; Smithsonian Institution, 2.

Text copyright © 1996 by Monica Kulling. Illustrations copyright © 1996 by Ying-Hwa Hu and Cornelius Van Wright. Maps copyright © 1996 by Random House, Inc. All rights reserved under International and Pan-American Copyright Conventions. Published in the United States by Random House, Inc., New York, and simultaneously in Canada by Random House of Canada Limited, Toronto.

http://www.randomhouse.com/

Library of Congress Cataloging-in-Publication Data
Kulling, Monica. Vanished! : the mysterious disappearance of Amelia Earhart / by Monica Kulling ; illustrated by Ying-Hwa Hu and Cornelius Van Wright. p. cm. — (Step into reading. A step 4 book) SUMMARY: Examines the mysterious disappearance of the world-famous woman pilot who was lost over the Pacific Ocean while on a historic round-the-world flight in 1937. ISBN 0-679-87124-1 (pbk.) — ISBN 0-679-97124-6 (lib. bdg.) 1. Earhart, Amelia, 1897–1937—Juvenile literature. 2. Missing persons—Juvenile literature. 3. Women air pilots—United States—Biography—Juvenile literature. [1. Earhart, Amelia, 1897–1937. 2. Air pilots. 3. Women—Biography.] I. Hu, Ying-Hwa, ill. II. Van Wright, Cornelius, ill. III. Title. IV. Series: Step into reading. Step 4 book. TL540.E3K85 1996 629.13'092—dc20 [B] 95-26854
Printed in the United States of America 10 9 8 7 6 5 4 3 2 1

STEP INTO READING is a trademark of Random House, Inc.

For Judy, a Zonta girl — MK

Mayday! Mayday!

July 2, 1937, 6:15 a.m.

The *Electra* is in trouble.

The silver plane has flown for nineteen hours without a stop. High above the Pacific Ocean, it is running out of gas!

Amelia Earhart is at the controls. She is an expert pilot. Her record-setting flights have made her famous all over the world.

Earhart is trying to set a new record. She is trying to fly around the Earth at its widest point—the equator!

No one has ever tried it, and many people say that it cannot be done. It is a 29,000-mile trip over wild jungles, empty deserts, and vast oceans. A pilot could easily get lost along the way.

*Amelia Earhart and Fred Noonan review the route
of their round-the-world flight one last time.*

Fred Noonan is Amelia Earhart's navigator. It is his job to help Earhart stay on
course. So far they have traveled 22,000
miles—nearly three-quarters of the way
around the world!

It has taken them thirty-two days. They
have landed in more than a dozen foreign
countries. Finally, they are in the home-

stretch. They are due to arrive in America on July 4, and a huge celebration is planned.

But this last leg of their trip is the most dangerous. Earhart and Noonan are flying from Lae, New Guinea, to Oakland, California—some 7,000 miles across the gigantic Pacific Ocean.

The *Electra* cannot hold enough gas for such a long flight, so the fliers must stop to refuel. There is a fresh supply of gas waiting for them on Howland Island. But can they find it?

Howland Island is a tiny speck of land just one mile long and a half mile wide. It would be difficult to find on a good day. And today there is thick fog, heavy rain, and strong winds.

"*Itasca* from Earhart. *Itasca* from Earhart. Give me the weather. I've got to know the weather!"

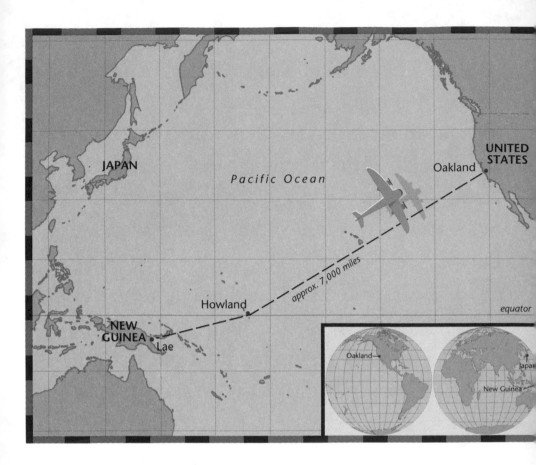

Far below, on the choppy waters of the Pacific, Amelia Earhart's voice crackles over the radio of the U.S. Coast Guard ship *Itasca.*

The *Itasca* is standing by to assist Earhart. The ship has been instructed to send her weather reports and other information that will help her reach the island.

But there is a problem. The ship's radio operator cannot get a message through to Earhart. He has been trying for hours without success. He can hear her, but she cannot hear him!

Earhart's voice comes over the radio again. She sounds tired and desperate.

"We are circling, but cannot hear you. Gas is running low!"

The *Itasca* crew searches the sky anxiously for signs of the plane. The radio operator keeps sending messages. He knows that if he doesn't make contact soon, the *Electra* will crash.

Earhart's voice comes over the radio one last time.

"We are running north and south—"

Then the line goes dead.

The *Electra* has vanished.

*Amelia with her close friend First Lady Eleanor Roosevelt.
One night, at a fancy White House party, Amelia found out
that Eleanor had never flown. The two ladies sneaked out
of the party and took a late-night flight over Washington,
dressed in their white gloves and evening gowns.*

America's Flying Sweetheart

When Amelia Earhart disappeared, she was the most famous woman in America. Everyone knew the daring pilot with the shy smile. Her face appeared on billboards and magazine covers. Her name was used to advertise everything from cars to luggage to pajamas. She was even good friends with President Roosevelt and his wife, Eleanor!

Amelia was born in Atchison, Kansas, on July 24, 1897. She saw her first plane at the Iowa State Fair when she was ten years old. It was made of wood, wire, and canvas. It looked like a giant kite!

Amelia wasn't impressed by that first plane. But years later, she saw a plane that changed her life.

Amelia went with a friend to watch a stunt-flying show. A pilot at the show decided to scare the two girls. He flew his plane straight at them. Amelia's friend ran, but Amelia did not move a muscle. At the last minute, the pilot pulled back the control stick and flew over her head.

"I believe that little red airplane said something to me as it swished by," Amelia said later.

Amelia decided she had to fly one of those machines. She got a job and put every penny toward flying lessons. By the time she was twenty-five, she had her pilot's

Amelia saw a plane for the first time when she was ten years old...

license. She was one of only a dozen women in the world with a license to fly.

But Amelia wasn't content just to fly.

She wanted to go higher and faster than anyone else.

Amelia set her first air record just a few months after she got her license. She

...and fifteen years later, she became a pilot. This is the photo from her first pilot's license.

flew her plane straight up to an altitude of 14,000 feet—nearly three miles—before the engine quit. Amelia had to land with the power off, but she had her record!

Even though Amelia was a skilled pilot, she couldn't get a job flying airplanes. Pilot jobs were scarce, especially for women. Soon her money ran out, and she was forced to sell her plane.

Then, in 1928, Amelia received a phone call. A wealthy woman named Amy Phipps Guest was sponsoring a flight across the Atlantic Ocean. She wanted a woman to be on board. No woman had ever crossed the Atlantic in an airplane.

Amelia jumped at the chance. Even though she would only be a passenger on the flight, it would still be an incredible adventure.

The *Friendship* took off from Trepassey,

Amelia shakes hands with Amy Phipps Guest, the woman who sponsored the Friendship *flight.*

Newfoundland, on June 17, 1928, with Amelia aboard. After two days of stormy weather—and with less than an hour's

New York City throws a ticker-tape parade in honor of Amelia (in the front car) *and the rest of the* Friendship *crew.*

worth of gas left—the plane touched down in Burry Port, Wales. Amelia Earhart had become the first woman to cross the Atlantic by air!

Amelia was famous overnight. Crowds of people gathered to see her. Kings and

queens invited her to dine. The President of the United States sent a telegram to congratulate her.

Back home, Amelia was greeted by a huge ticker-tape parade in New York City. But she didn't think she deserved all the attention. She hadn't even flown the plane! Amelia told reporters that she had been nothing more than "a sack of potatoes" on the flight. But she vowed that someday she would fly across the Atlantic Ocean on her own.

A publisher named George P. Putnam asked Amelia to write a book about the *Friendship* flight. The book was a huge success. Amelia made enough money to buy a new plane, and before long she was setting records again.

She became the first woman to fly solo across the United States and back. She became the first woman to fly solo across the Pacific Ocean. And, just as she said she would, she became the first woman to fly solo across the Atlantic Ocean.

By 1936, Amelia was a celebrity. She was also a hero, especially to young women.

Amelia Earhart with George P. Putnam. After he published her book, George asked Amelia to marry him. She said no. George proposed four more times, and four more times Amelia refused. Finally, on the sixth proposal, she said yes. Amelia and George were married in Noank, Connecticut, on February 4, 1931.

She spoke at schools across the country, and everywhere she went, she told girls they should not be afraid to follow their dreams. "Women must try to do things, as men have tried," she said. "When they fail, their failure must be but a challenge to others."

Amelia talks about flying to a group of girls and boys in Newark, New Jersey.

Amelia Earhart had already made history. She could have stopped flying, but there was one more flight she wanted to make.

At a press conference in 1937, she told reporters: "Well, I've seen the Atlantic, and I've seen the Pacific, too. Just say I want to fly around the globe at its waistline."

Her fans thought the round-the-world flight would be just another first for Amelia Earhart. They did not dream it would be her last.

Searching for Amelia Earhart

Soon after Earhart's last radio message, the biggest air and sea search in history begins. President Roosevelt sends 4,000 troops, ten ships, and sixty-five planes to look for Earhart and Noonan.

But the Pacific Ocean is vast, and much of it is controlled by the Japanese. The

United States and Japan are not on friendly terms. A world war is brewing, and neither country trusts the other.

The U.S. Navy asks permission to search Japanese waters. The Japanese government refuses. They say they will search those areas themselves.

After sixteen days, there is still no sign of the *Electra* or its two passengers. The Navy calls off the search. They determine that the plane crashed and sank somewhere in the Pacific Ocean. They report that Earhart and Noonan are dead.

The news stuns the world. How could the "First Lady of the Air" just disappear? Where is her plane? Where is her body?

Some people are not convinced that Amelia is dead. Maybe she crashed on a deserted island. Maybe she is waiting to be rescued!

Excitement grows as ham radio operators in California and Hawaii pick up SOS signals from the South Pacific. They say the signals are coming from the *Electra*. Is Earhart alive and trying to get help?

Still other people think Amelia didn't crash at all. She often joked that she would

This picture is believed to be the last photograph ever taken of Amelia Earhart and Fred Noonan (far right). It was snapped at Lae, New Guinea, just minutes before the fliers took off for Howland Island.

like to sneak away to "a nice quiet stretch of beach somewhere." Has she finally done it?

Soon everyone in America is talking about the Amelia Earhart mystery. The newspapers are full of it. But then an even bigger story comes along: World War II.

At first, the U.S. stays out of the war. But on December 7, 1941, the Japanese attack Pearl Harbor, the site of a U.S. Navy base. Suddenly, America is swept into the fighting. People forget all about Amelia Earhart as the war takes center stage.

Then, two years later, RKO Studios releases a movie called *Flight for Freedom.* The movie is about a female pilot on a flight around the world. In the movie, the pilot agrees to get "lost" on purpose. The Navy goes to the Pacific Ocean and pretends to search for her. But they are really spying on the Japanese.

The movie sounds a lot like the Amelia Earhart story. Before long, the mystery is back in the spotlight. Was Earhart working for the U.S. Navy? Was her round-the-world trip part of a top-secret spy operation?

The Navy quickly denies the rumors.

They say Earhart was *not* working for the military. She was *not* spying on the Japanese when her plane went down.

But a few years later, Earhart's mother, Amy Otis Earhart, tells the press something shocking.

"Amelia told me many things," she says. "But there were some things she couldn't tell me. I am convinced that she was on some sort of government mission."

Earhart's own mother thinks she was a spy!

Amelia Earhart: Spy?

In 1960, a woman named Josephine Blanco Akiyama comes forward. Akiyama is from Saipan, a small island in the Pacific. Saipan was controlled by the Japanese during World War II.

Akiyama says she saw two American pilots, a man and a woman, on Saipan in 1937. The pilots had crashed nearby and been captured by Japanese soldiers.

Is the story true? Were the two pilots Amelia Earhart and Fred Noonan? If so, what were they doing at Saipan? It is more than 2,000 miles away from Howland Island!

A reporter named Fred Goerner decides to investigate. He goes to Saipan and speaks to hundreds of people. Some say they saw

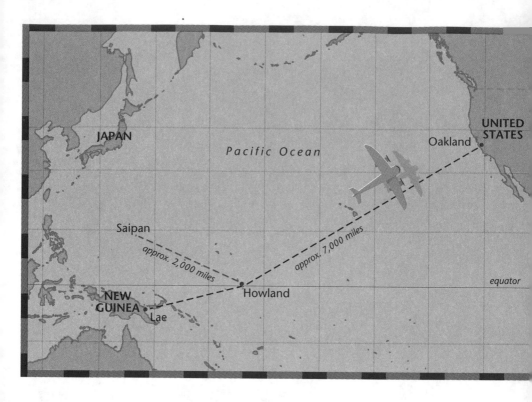

the pilots, too. Others say they heard stories about them—that they were shot to death, or that they died in prison. One man says he even knows where the pilots are buried! He takes Goerner to the place.

Goerner digs up the gravesite. He uncovers the remains of eight people. But none of the skulls or teeth match either Amelia's or Fred's.

Then a retired U.S. Marine named Everett Henson, Jr., calls Goerner. He tells Goerner that he was stationed on Saipan during the war. In July 1944, his captain ordered him to dig up two bodies from an unmarked grave. The captain told Henson that the bodies belonged to Amelia Earhart and Fred Noonan!

The skeletons were placed in two metal containers. After that, Henson never saw them again.

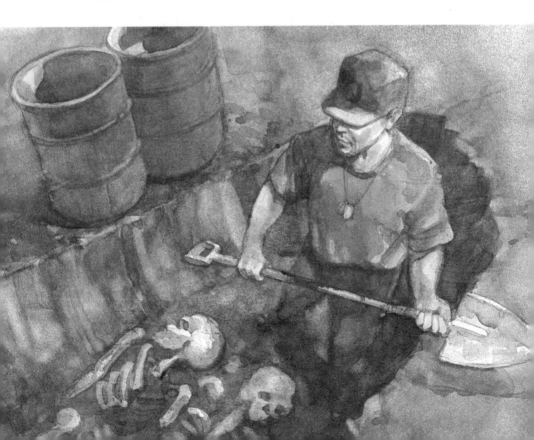

By now, Goerner is convinced that Earhart was on Saipan. But how can he prove it? If he cannot find her body, perhaps he can find her plane.

Goerner and his team drag the harbor at Saipan. They find about a hundred pounds of wreckage on the bottom. The rusted metal is covered in slime and coral. When the pieces are cleaned, they turn out to be from an airplane! Is it the *Electra*?

Goerner takes a piece back to the U.S. He shows it to an airplane technician named Paul Mantz. Mantz was in charge of preparing the *Electra* for the round-the-world flight. If anyone could identify a piece of the plane, it would be him.

Mantz examines the piece. He says it looks familiar. But when he takes it apart, he discovers that it was made in Japan. The plane Goerner found is not the *Electra*.

After six years of searching, Goerner still cannot prove that Earhart and Noonan crashed at Saipan. But he is sure they were there.

Goerner publishes a book called *The Search for Amelia Earhart*. In it, he describes what he thinks happened to Earhart. The book shocks many people.

Goerner believes that President Roosevelt approached Earhart before her round-the-world trip. He asked her to do something very important and very dangerous for her country. He asked her to be a spy!

Goerner says that Earhart agreed. Instead of flying straight to Howland Island from Lae, she made a detour. She flew over Japanese territory and took photographs with a hidden camera in her plane.

Then, on the way back to Howland Island, Earhart hit bad weather. She couldn't receive signals from the *Itasca* because she was too far away. Her plane ran out of gas and crashed.

Goerner thinks that Earhart and Noonan

were captured at Saipan by the Japanese. There they were either shot or thrown into prison for spying.

Parts of Goerner's story ring true. Earhart was a close friend of the Roosevelts. She wasn't afraid of taking risks. And, according to a mechanic named Robert T. Elliott, she did have a secret camera in the belly of her plane! Elliott claims to have installed the camera himself.

Goerner's theory explains how Earhart and Noonan could have wound up on Saipan Island. But is it true? Was Amelia Earhart really on a spy mission in 1937?

Amelia Earhart:
Prisoner of War?

There are some people who do not believe that Amelia Earhart was a spy. Retired U.S. Air Force officer Vincent Loomis is one of them.

Loomis spends twenty years investigating Earhart's disappearance. During his investigation, he meets a man named Bilimon Amaran. Amaran worked at a military hospital on the island of Jaluit in 1937. Like Saipan, Jaluit was controlled by the Japanese.

Amaran tells Loomis that a plane crashed in the ocean near Jaluit that summer. He saw the plane on the back of a Japanese ship. One of its wings was broken.

Amaran says he was asked to treat two

American pilots who were injured in the crash. One of them was a woman. He remembers her clearly. She was the first female pilot he had ever seen! She was very tall, with short, light brown hair. She wore pants like a man's, and she had a scarf tied around her neck.

Loomis is excited. Amaran's description fits Amelia Earhart perfectly!

Loomis talks to many other people on Jaluit. Their stories match what Amaran told him. He becomes convinced that the *Electra* crashed near Jaluit—*not* near Saipan.

Jaluit is much closer to Howland Island than Saipan. But it is still about 1,000 miles away. Loomis wonders how Earhart could have flown so far off course by accident. Wouldn't Noonan tell her she was heading in the wrong direction?

Then Loomis discovers that Noonan

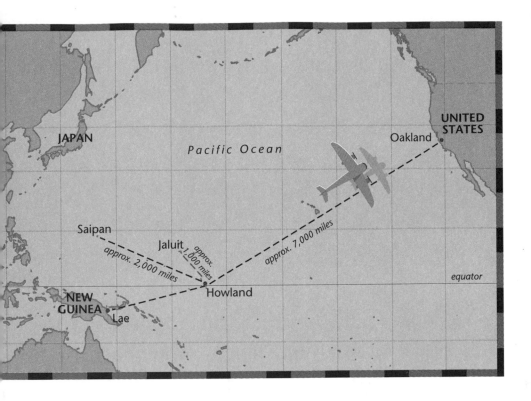

had a problem. He was an alcoholic. Only months before he became Earhart's navigator, he lost his job at Pan American Airways because of drinking.

Noonan had promised Earhart that he would stay sober during the flight, but he did not keep his promise. Halfway through the trip, he started drinking again.

Loomis thinks Noonan had been drinking the day the *Electra* took off for Howland Island. Earhart realized that Noonan could not navigate the plane properly, but she didn't want to turn back. Instead, she decided to find Howland herself.

Earhart was an excellent pilot, but she was not a trained navigator. She did not know how to use the tracking instruments on her plane. And because of the terrible weather, she could not rely on the stars to guide her. Earhart was flying blind!

Loomis believes that Earhart got lost

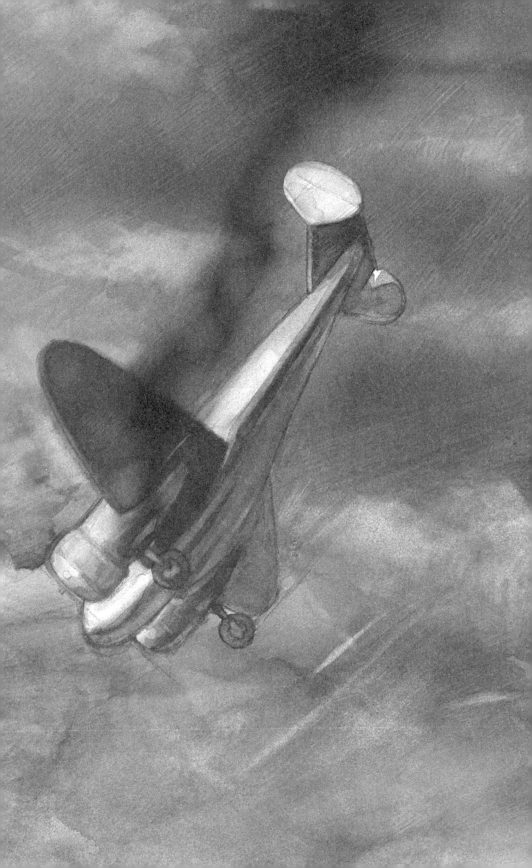

and flew into Japanese territory by mistake. Her plane ran out of gas and crashed near Jaluit. Then, even though she and Noonan were not spies, they were taken prisoner by the Japanese.

Loomis gains access to Japanese military

records from 1937. He makes an important discovery. The Japanese government told the U.S. Navy they would search for the *Electra*. They even gave the Navy a list of ships that would participate in the search. But those ships were never sent out!

Loomis thinks the Japanese government did not bother looking for Earhart because they knew exactly where she was. She was their prisoner of war!

Loomis publishes a book about his theory called *Amelia Earhart: The Final Story*. But is it the final story?

Is Loomis right? Was Amelia Earhart an innocent victim of the war?

Is Goerner right? Was she captured as a spy?

Is the Navy right? Did she drown at sea?

Or are they all wrong?

What happened to Amelia Earhart on July 2, 1937?
We may never know.

Amelia Earhart Lives

In 1970, a man named Joe Klaas writes a book called *Amelia Earhart Lives*. In the book, Klaas claims that he knows where Earhart is. He says she is living in New Jersey, disguised as a housewife named Irene Bolam.

Irene Bolam does look a great deal like Amelia Earhart. She also flies airplanes. But she insists that she is not the missing pilot. She sues the publisher of the book and wins. The book is taken out of the stores.

- For all we know, Amelia Earhart may still be alive—though she would be nearly 100 years old today.

No one has ever found her body. No one

has ever found her plane. And until that happens, her disappearance will remain an unsolved mystery.

But no matter how or why Amelia Earhart disappeared, she will not be forgotten. Her daring flights helped open up the sky to modern-day air travel. And her strength and courage continue to inspire both men and women everywhere.

Amelia waves good-bye before her final flight.

Date Due	Borrower's Name	Regis-trar

921
EAR

Kulling, Monica
Vanished!

GAYLORD F